Pet Detectives
Tortoise Trouble

Written by Jana Hunter

Illustrated by Kim Blundell

Lost a pet? Seen a pet crime?

Then you need the Pet Detectives!

Why?

Pet Detectives find pets.

They stop crime.

How do I know?

I am a Pet Detective!

Chapter One

Let me tell you about my latest case …
It started like any other Monday.
I got up. I got dressed.
Then the doorbell rang.
"Uh, oh! Trouble!"
I pulled on my detective's hat and ran to the door …

Uh, oh!

A kid in a tortoise-print T-shirt stood there.
"You must help me!" she cried. "I'm Kara and
I've lost my Rocket."
"Rocket?" I pointed to my sign. "I do pets."
"I know," said Kara. "I can read."
This kid was clever.

4

"Go on …" I said.

"I lost my Rocket yesterday," she sniffed.

"Did it zoom off into space?"

Kara looked puzzled. "My Rocket doesn't zoom.
He plods."

Now I was puzzled. "What kind of rocket plods?"

"A tortoise," Kara said.

"A tortoise?" I laughed. "Named …
ROCKET!" we shouted, laughing.

6

Then I remembered I was on a case.

"Ahem …" I flipped open my notebook. "Give me the facts."

Kara began. "I was helping my dad build his rockery."

"Where?"

Kara rolled her eyes. "In the garden, of course."

"Just the facts," I reminded her.

"Okay," Kara nodded.
"One minute Rocket was munching on a cabbage leaf
.. next minute he was gone!"
"And the cabbage leaf?"
"That was gone too," said Kara.

Gone!

"Have you got a picture of Rocket?"
Kara nodded. "At home."
"Let's go!"

Chapter Two

I went over the facts ...

Number One: Tortoise shells are pretty.

"Maybe Rocket has been turned into a pair of
sunglasses, or a comb. "
"They're made of plastic, now," said Kara.
(I told you the kid was clever.)

Number two: Tortoises are slow.

"Maybe Rocket was hit by a car, zooming down the motorway."

Kara rolled her eyes, again. "We live in a village, remember?"

Okay, so there are no motorways in our village.

But animals can sometimes travel a long way.

(I know – I'm a Pet Detective.)

"Are there any goats
nearby?" I asked, when
we got to Kara's house.

"Goats?" said Kara, opening the door to her room.
"Yes, goats ... Wow!" I stared into the room.
There were tortoises everywhere – posters, books,
lamps, even a tortoise-shaped rug!

I looked at Rocket's picture. His shell was patterned brown and black and he had very tasty looking wrinkly legs.
"Goats will eat anything," I told Kara.
"There aren't any goats," said Kara. "But there is a dog … a big dog. And he lives next door!"
"Let's go."

Kara was right. Next door's dog was big – really big.
But he had no teeth!
"This dog couldn't bite a jelly!" I joked.
"You're right," laughed Kara.
Suddenly a toy flew out from the pram.
"But that baby can throw!" I said.

Woof!

"If that baby threw Rocket," I said, "he will be here somewhere."
(Detectives can work out things like that.)

So we searched next door's garden.
We found lots of toys ... but no tortoise.

There was only one thing to do – return to
the scene of the crime. So back we went to Kara's garden.

Chapter Three

"No sign of a struggle here,"
I said, looking round Kara's
garden.

But I'm a detective.
And detectives know that things
are not always as they seem.
So I looked at the rockery.

Hmmm ...

Then I looked at it more closely ...
"How slow does Rocket move?" I asked.

"Really slow," said Kara.

"Really, really slow?"

Kara nodded. "Why?"

"Well, that rock is moving all by itself."

We looked. The rock was patterned brown and black.
And it was moving slowly.

"That's not a rock," we shouted. "It's ...

ROCKET!"

"Rocket," said Kara, "you were here all the time ..."

"... cleverly disguised as a rock," I added.
(Detectives know about disguises.)

"I told you Rocket was slow," said Kara.
She was clever, this kid ...
... and so am I.
"Case solved," I said.

What a Pet Detective needs

notebook

detective's hat

brains

book

magnifying glass

1 brains – to think cases through

2 detective's hat – to keep brains warm

3 notebook – to write down the facts

4 magnifying glass – to look at the clues

5 a book called 'Pets'

6 ... and a case to solve

✿ Ideas for guided reading ✿

Learning objectives: Use awareness of grammar to decipher unfamiliar words; read on sight high frequency words; read text aloud with intonation and expression appropriate to the grammar and punctuation; work effectively in groups by ensuring group members take a turn, challenging, supporting and moving on.

Curriculum links: Science: plants and animals in the local environment

Interest words: tortoise, detective, rockery, disguised

Resources: an envelope with the answer to the mystery inside

Word count: 669

Getting started

- Begin by asking the children to take turns saying what they know about detectives. Add that this story is about a pet detective and discuss the title.
- In pairs, ask the children to predict what the trouble is with the tortoise. Have a 'Cluedo' style envelope prepared with the answer written inside *(Kara couldn't find her tortoise because the rockery disguised him)*. Tell the children you will reveal this at the end.
- Ask them to read the blurb silently. Discuss the two types of punctuation used (full stop and exclamation mark). Ask the children to explain how punctuation affects the way they read.

Reading and responding

- Read pp2-3 as a group, focusing on the effects of punctuation. Ask the children to discuss the strategies they use if they come to a tricky word. Remind them that they can leave a gap and read on, to work out words.
- Ask the group to read on silently to p21. Encourage them to try and solve the mystery themselves – before the Pet Detective does! They will need to read carefully to get all the facts.
- Listen to individuals read aloud in turn. Remind them that punctuation will help them use good expression when reading aloud. Observe how the children solve tricky words. Do they use a range of strategies?